D0975004

Welcome to the Fairy House –
a whole new magical world…

Look for all *The Fairy House* books:

FAIRY FRIENDS

FAIRY FOR A DAY

FAIRIES TO THE RESCUE

FAIRY RIDING SCHOOL

Kelly McKain

Illustrated by Nicola Slater

SCHOLASTIC

New York Toronto London Auckland Sydney
Mexico City New Delhi Hong Kong Buenos Aires

ISBN 13: 978-0-545-04237-6
ISBN 10: 0-545-04237-2

12 11 10 9 8 7 6 5 4 3 2 1 7 8 9 10 11 12/0
Printed in China
First Scholastic U.S.A. printing, August 2007

For

Jill, Katie, and Lew the Chew, with love

With thanks to

Amanda Punter, Katy Moran, Elaine McQuade, Andrew Biscomb, Georgia Lawe, Sarah Spedding, Kate Wilson, Claire Tagg, Eleanor Schramm, and Hilary Murray-Hill for working your magic on this, and for loving the Fairy House as much as I do! xx

Chapter 1

Katie twisted the ring Aunt Jane had given her around and around on her finger, as she always did when she was nervous. The package just *had* to come today.

At last she heard the mailman crunching his way up the gravel driveway, but she was much too shy to go running up to him. Instead she listened to her mom answering the door, and to the mailman asking how they were settling in.

They'd only been in the new house two weeks.

The new house really was a *new* house — it had just been built. Katie found it strange that no one had ever used the stove or the bathtub before they got there. The house looked exactly the same as all the others in the small housing development, except that her mom had painted the front door a bright pink. In the fairy tales Katie loved reading, the houses always had secret passageways or hidden cupboards to explore. But in their own house, every single nook and cranny was crammed with their things.

As soon as she heard the front door closing, Katie hurried into the hall. She didn't have to ask if the package had come — her mom was clutching a large brown-paper-wrapped box!

Katie knew it was what she'd been waiting for. A new house of her very own.

The moment her mom put the box down Katie pounced on it and tore off the paper. She could feel her heart pounding as she wrenched the box open, reached

inside, and pulled out the contents. There it was, the dollhouse!

It was made of pink plastic with little cut-out windows and it had a yellow door with a tiny blue handle. Katie unhooked a latch on the roof and the whole front of the house swung open. Inside was a kitchen and living room, and stairs to the bedrooms above. "Four bedrooms! Just like our house," she cried, then added, "I mean, our old house."

"There's more inside the box," said Katie's mom.

Katie reached in

again and rummaged around. She fished out packet after packet of tiny furniture — a sofa, beds, a table, dressers, kitchen cupboards, and a grand piano.

Katie traced her hand over the pink-tiled plastic roof — it was finally here, her very own dollhouse! She'd been thinking and even dreaming about one for what seemed like forever — and asking and asking and asking, of course! Even though it wasn't anywhere near her birthday, Katie's mom had finally given in and said she could have one for being so helpful with the move.

Together they set out all the doll-house furniture on the table. "There's everything you need to make a lovely home right here," said Katie's mom.

"Yes, it's great, it's just a little plain, that's all," Katie murmured. She thought for a moment, then had an idea. "Oh, I know!" she cried. "I can make it unusual, so there's only one like it in the whole world. I'll paint the door, and make curtains, and draw pictures to go on the walls, just like you did with our house!"

Katie's mom was an artist, so she really had created the brightly colored paintings that hung on their walls.

"Great idea," said Katie's mom. "Look, it's a lovely day, why don't you take everything outside and get some fresh air?"

So Katie ran upstairs and grabbed her paints and brushes and stickers

and glitter and glue. She scooped up a handful of Barbies, too, then realized they'd be far too big to fit into the dollhouse. Katie stopped — she hadn't even thought about *dolls*. What good was a dollhouse if she had no dolls to actually live in it? Then she was struck with another great idea — she'd make some!

Katie picked up some pieces of cardboard from her desk (Katie's mom always cut up the old cereal boxes for her), and her school pencil case with the scissors and markers inside. She ran downstairs

and rummaged in the craft drawer for the bag of fabric scraps. She could use them to dress her dolls, and make curtains, and maybe even bedspreads! Katie's heart was pounding again — who wanted a stuffy old dollhouse that was already perfect anyway? This would be much more fun!

Katie put all her things inside the pink plastic house, shut the latch, and picked it up by the handle, just like a suitcase. Then she headed outside. The backyard was just a neat rectangle of grass, though Katie's mom was planning to plant bushes, ivy, and maybe even a vegetable garden. The developers had only put two thin strips of wire up between the yards, but the neighbors had already replaced theirs with a newly painted wooden fence. Katie's mom liked the open feel and kept the wire along

the back edge of the yard. It was easy for Katie to duck underneath and explore beyond the fence.

Beyond the wire was a patch of rough ground that hadn't been built on yet. It wasn't really big enough to call a meadow, but the grass was high and full of daisies, dandelions, and violets. At the center stood a grand old oak tree. Katie had discovered it the day they moved in. It was the perfect place for daydreaming, playing, and making things. Since no one else ever went there, Katie was starting to think of it as her own special, private place. She swished through the grass and set the dollhouse down under the tree, then she clicked it open and pulled out her art things.

And there, with the breeze rustling the leaves above her and insects buzzing happily around, Katie spent a lovely morning making the dollhouse her very own. First, she painted the front door a bright purple. Then, she stuck silver heart and star stickers on the plain pink furniture and arranged it in the different rooms, singing her favorite songs as she worked.

Next, she started on the cardboard dolls, drawing outlines of the shapes and then cutting carefully around them. She made four — one for each bedroom. Then she tipped her bag of fabric scraps out onto the ground and chose the material for their outfits. Two were getting jeans and two were going to have cute skirts and tops. The cardboard dolls would have parties in the house all the time, Katie decided. She'd make them little paper hats and decorations and even tiny games to play!

Planning her dolls' first party was a lot of fun — but it made her feel lonely, too. She wished she had someone to

share it with, but her old friends were all back in the city getting ready for the school play. It was so unfair — she had been cast as the lead, but because of the move to the country, she was missing it all.

Her new school wasn't *that* bad, she supposed, but she found everything there so new and strange — their math books were blue instead of orange, the cafeteria smelled different, and recess was much too short. Her teacher, Mrs. Borthwick, was a big, cheerful lady who wore thick tights and had a short gray bob. Most of the children seemed nice, too, but she hadn't made any real friends yet. She missed having girls to whisper secrets to and make presents for and play games with.

I hope I find a friend before the summer

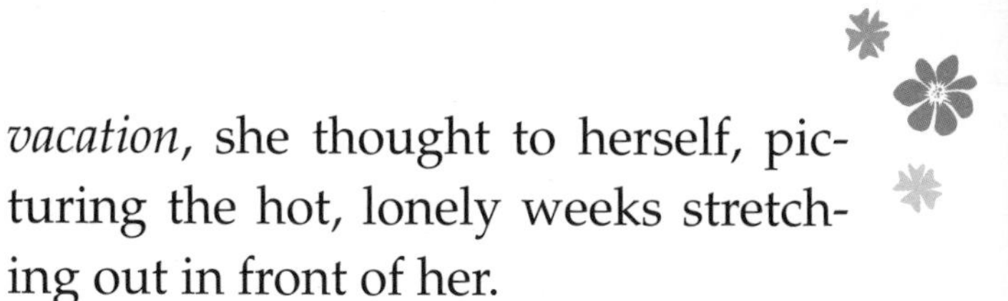

vacation, she thought to herself, picturing the hot, lonely weeks stretching out in front of her.

For a moment, Katie had the strangest feeling, as if she were being watched. She glanced all around her, but no one was there. She shrugged and began cutting out a striped skirt and singing a new song, the one about the kookaburra and the old gum tree. She didn't even get to the second verse before she heard her mom calling her in for lunch.

Her mom sounded so worried that Katie instantly leaped up, shouting, "Here I am! Over the fence!" She hurried inside, but she planned to come back out as soon as lunch was over.

But once she'd eaten her sandwich and helped her mom clean up they had to go visit her Aunt Jane. The

three of them ended up going for a long walk and then had dinner. When they got home it was already bath time. By the time Katie's mom had detangled and dried Katie's long brown hair, it was past bedtime and she said "Lights out right now," so there was no time for a story. Just as she was falling asleep, Katie remembered that the dollhouse was still under the oak tree. But she was too tired to get up again and bring it in — so that's where it stayed.

First thing the next morning, Katie wanted to get back to work on her

dollhouse project — there were the dolls' outfits to finish, and she hadn't even started on the curtains. She gave her mom a good morning hug and tried to hurry out the back door — but her mom insisted she have a bowl of cereal first! Soon enough, though, Katie was outside, slipping under the wire fence and making her way across the almost-meadow to the oak tree.

And that's when she got a huge surprise. Her cardboard dolls were lying on the ground by the front door — but she was sure she'd left them safely in their bedrooms inside the dollhouse.

Stranger still, there were blue polka-dot curtains hanging in one of the bedroom windows.

Curtains she hadn't made.

Katie felt her stomach flip over. Had someone been here overnight,

playing with her things? Suddenly, something caught her attention. Strange sounds. Almost like *voices*. She froze, listening. But all she could hear were birds singing in the trees and insects buzzing through the flowers.

But . . . aha! There it was again! Definitely voices, she was sure now. At first Katie thought they were coming from far away, but then she realized that they were very *close*, but just very *tiny*. They sounded beautiful — almost magical — like

crystal wind chimes tinkling in the breeze.

Katie listened hard. She gasped. The voices were *right beside her*.

They were coming from *inside* the dollhouse.

Chapter 2

Katie lay down on her stomach and peered through the kitchen window. She gasped in amazement. She blinked and stared and blinked again.

She absolutely and utterly could NOT believe her eyes. Inside the kitchen were four tiny creatures with shimmering wings and beautiful, silky petal skirts!

Fairies!

But how could that be? It just wasn't possible! Katie knew that fairies existed only in books, not in real life! And yet here they were, in her very own dollhouse! Could they really have thrown her cardboard dolls out onto the grass and moved in themselves?!

Feeling excitement pounding in her chest, Katie crept closer and listened hard. The fairies seemed to be arguing. "But we haven't even been given a *task*!" yelled the one with the dazzling blue hair. "It's just so *unfair*!" And she stamped her foot to prove it.

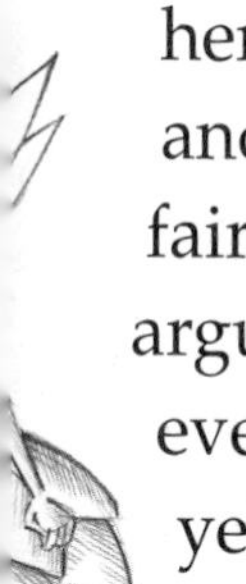

Another shook her long fiery-orange locks and cried, "Maybe we don't *deserve* a task, after the way we behaved. Maybe we've been banished from Fairyland forever!"

The blonde fairy twirled one of her braids around her finger anxiously. Katie noticed that, instead of elastics, they were tied up with tiny daisies. "Oh, no, that can't be true!" she said gently. "I'm sure we'll be given a chance to prove we're sorry. She wouldn't just send us away forever and ever . . . would she?"

They all fell silent then, looking horrified at the thought. They turned to the thin, fragile fairy with the jet-black hair, but she stayed silent, looking down and scuffing the sole of her tiny turquoise shoe against the plastic floor.

The other three burst to life again, all shouting at once. Katie coughed loudly, but not one single fairy turned in her direction. "Hello!" she called. But still nothing.

Katie decided that if she didn't do something drastic, she'd never get their attention. She leaned forward and put her hand over the kitchen window, which made the room completely dark. *That* certainly made them notice her!

There were cries of "Eeek!" and "Help!" and "What's happening?!"

Katie took her hand away to find

four frightened fairy faces staring out at her. "Oh, sorry! I didn't mean to scare you!" she said.

But the fairies stayed silent, staring. The flame-haired one was trembling and the one with the beautiful purple skirt gripped her friend's arm in fright. "Y-y-you can see us?" she stammered.

"That means she must believe in fairies!" gasped the blue-haired one, staring wide-eyed at her friends.

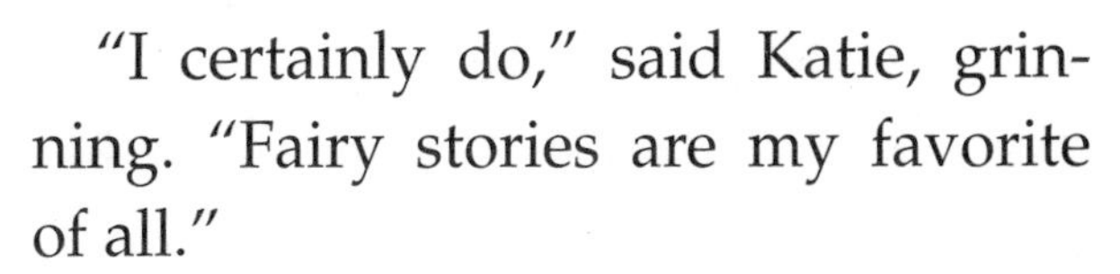

"I certainly do," said Katie, grinning. "Fairy stories are my favorite of all."

Katie suddenly remembered what her mom said to do when she met new people. "I'm Katie; it's nice to meet you," she said, in her most polite voice. She held out her hand for them to shake and then realized it wouldn't fit through the window, so she poked her little finger through instead. The fairies all leaped back in alarm. Then the one with the daisy braids stepped forward and shook Katie's finger.

"I'm Daisy," she said, "and these are

my friends — Bluebell, Rosehip, and Snowdrop." She waved first toward the blue-haired fairy, then to the bright-orange-haired one, and finally to the jet-black-haired one, who gave Katie a nervous smile.

"This is amazing!" Katie exclaimed. "I didn't know you existed in real life."

"We don't actually live here on earth," Daisy explained. "Fairies only come to the human world to do tasks for the Fairy Queen."

"What kind of tasks?" asked Katie. She hadn't read about anything like this in her *Illustrated Treasury of Fairy Stories*.

"Things like helping flowers to grow and picking up litter," Rosehip told her. "The fairies come and do their tasks, and then they go home and get a reward."

"But *we're* not going home," wailed Bluebell. "We were sent here because we always argue with one another. Fairies only go home when they've done their task, and we haven't even been *given* a task, so how can we *do* one? How can we go home? We'll be stuck here forever and ever and we'll never see Fairyland again!"

That was when Snowdrop started sobbing quietly to herself. Daisy rushed over and put her arm around her. "Snowdrop, what's wrong?" she asked gently.

Snowdrop sniffled and clung tightly to Daisy. "Uh, it's just that, well, we *were* given a task," she mumbled.

Rosehip gasped and Bluebell stared. "What? When?" they demanded.

Daisy glared at them and they fell silent. "Why didn't you tell us?" she asked Snowdrop gently.

"The Fairy Queen gave it to me just as we were leaving," Snowdrop sniffled. "You'd already gone sliding down into the sparkling whirlwind to leave Fairyland, so you didn't see."

"Well, that's *good*, isn't it?" reasoned Bluebell. "We just have to do the task and then we can go home! Easy breezy!"

Snowdrop burst into fresh sobs. "But it's too *hard*," she wailed. "We'll never be able to do it. That's why I kept it a secret. It's the biggest task any fairy has ever been given, and I mean EVER! Look!" She rummaged in the purple petals of her skirt and thrust a piece of rolled up paper at Daisy, who unrolled it and read:

Fairy Task No. 45826

By Royal Command of the Fairy Queen

Terrible news has reached Fairyland. As you know, the Magic Oak is the gateway between Fairyland and the human world. The sparkling whirlwind can only drop fairies off *here*. Humans plan to knock down our special tree and build a house on the land. If this happens, fairies will no longer be able to come and help people and the environment. You must stop them from doing this terrible thing and make sure that the tree is protected for the future. Only then will you be allowed back into Fairyland.

By order of Her Eternal Majesty
The Fairy Queen

P.S. You will need one each of the twelve birthstones to work the magic that will save the tree—but hurry, there's not much time!

The fairies all stared at each other, stunned. For once there was absolute silence.

"See what I mean?" said Snowdrop, sniffling. She hung her head and her

shiny black hair fell forward over her tear-stained face.

"You're right — it's impossible!" cried Bluebell.

"And with no help at all, just this silly letter!" fumed Rosehip. The others gasped in shock and Rosehip's cheeks flushed red, clashing horribly with her hair. "Sorry, I didn't mean to criticize the Fairy Queen," she said quickly. She turned to the part of Katie she could see, which was precisely one eye and half a nose. "It's just, most fairies get some kind of instructions," she explained. "She hasn't even told us what birthstones *are*!"

Katie wished she could help, but she didn't know what birthstones were either.

Bluebell stamped her foot again, making all the little chairs around the kitchen table shake. "I bet she *wants*

us to fail, so she never has to see us again!"

"Now, now," said Daisy calmly. "You know that's not true, Bluebell. She's trusted us with the most important fairy task in the whole history of fairy tasks! We *have* to succeed. If we don't, the gateway between our worlds will be lost forever — that means the end of fairies helping humans!"

"Couldn't you use your fairy magic?" Katie asked, her huge voice was very loud in the tiny kitchen, making her feel like the giant in *Jack and the Beanstalk*. "Can't you make anything happen just by wishing it? Can't you simply use magic to get all

the birthstones here? Or better yet, just wish for the tree to be saved?"

The fairies all smiled at her sadly. "That's the problem with fairy stories written by humans," said Rosehip. "They all make us out to be superheroes. But we haven't got unlimited powers." She gestured to the kitchen table and Katie craned her neck to see a small bottle of sparkling dust sitting there. "We do have this fairy dust from the magic fountain in Fairyland, but we can only use it for small spells."

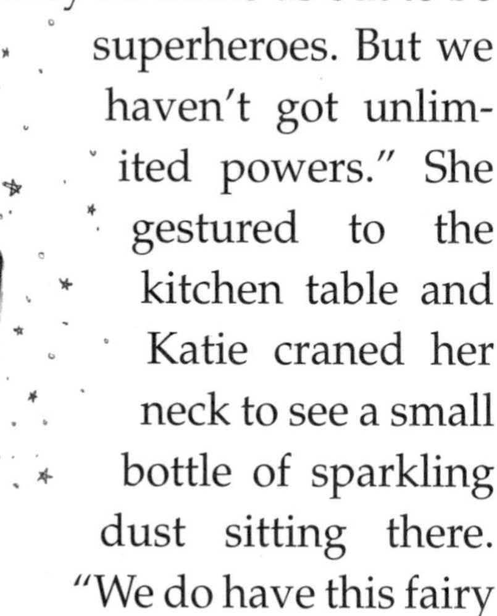

"Oh," said Katie. For once she didn't have any more good ideas.

"Even if we find out what birthstones are —" Bluebell began.

". . . and collect them all —" Rosehip added.

". . . we still don't know how to do the magic," Snowdrop finished.

With that the fairies all sank into a gloomy mood, wings drooping.

"I'd like to help," said Katie, "but it's difficult when I'm so big. I've got a tree root sticking into my ribs and a horrible crick in my neck."

Bluebell's eyes shone. "That's something we *can* fix," she said. She picked up the bottle of fairy dust and skipped out of the room.

A moment later the purple front door swung open and out she came. She pulled out the cork and tipped the bottle over.

"Careful," warned Daisy from the

window, "don't use too much, that's all we've got."

"I know; don't worry!" called Bluebell crossly. Katie watched as Bluebell carefully shook out a little of the sparkling dust on to the tiny blue door handle. What on earth was she planning to do?

"OK, you can shrink now," she told Katie triumphantly.

"What?!" Katie cried.

Bluebell grinned. "It's easy. All you have to do it put your little finger on

the door handle and say, 'I believe in fairies' three times. Then you'll shrink. That way you can be the same size as we are, and you can come into the house and help us figure out what to do and . . ."

But Katie had stopped listening. What if something went wrong and she couldn't get big again? What if she got small, but her clothes stayed big? Worst of all, what if she kept getting smaller and smaller and smaller until she was only a dot, then a speck, and then nothing at all? "I'm not sure," she mumbled.

Bluebell shrugged. "It's up to you."

Katie's head was full of worries. But she really, *really* wanted to go inside the dollhouse. She took a deep breath, squeezed her eyes shut, and put her little finger on the tiny door

handle. The other three fairies leaned out of the kitchen window to watch.

"I believe in fairies," Katie whispered. "I believe in fairies. I believe in fairies."

Chapter 3

The first thing Katie felt was a strange tingling at the top of her head, like someone had sprinkled fizzing baking powder on it. Then there was a huge whooshing sound, and suddenly everything around her was getting bigger and bigger and bigger. Except that it wasn't, of course. Actually, *she* was getting smaller and smaller and smaller. When she finally stopped shrinking she was the same size as Bluebell.

She looked around her at the dandelions, which now seemed as big as beach umbrellas. She smiled at Bluebell in amazement, and Bluebell grinned back. Then a low, sleepy buzzing filled the air. Katie whirled around to see a huge bumblebee coming right toward her. "Eeek!!!!!" she squealed, racing into the dollhouse and slamming the door shut.

The other fairies ran into the hall to greet her, giggling. "The bees won't hurt you," Daisy said. "Animals and insects love fairies."

"Yes, well, I'm *not* a fairy, am I?" cried Katie. "And I'd rather not find

out whether the bees can tell the difference!"

"I don't blame you!" said Rosehip.

Katie looked at Daisy's shimmering wings and bent her arm behind her, trying to feel whether or not she had any of her own. She was disappointed to find that she didn't.

"Sorry," said Snowdrop, "no wings. As you said, you didn't become a fairy."

"I wish I *could* be one!" said Katie. But then she realized that if she were a real fairy she'd have to go back to Fairyland with the others when they'd finished the task and that she wouldn't get to live with her mom — in fact, her mom wouldn't even be able to *see* her! She decided that shrinking and then getting big again was the best thing after all.

Katie was startled out of her

thoughts by Bluebell dashing inside and grabbing her hand. "Come on," she cried, "I want to show you what I did to my room."

"It's not *your* room!" said Rosehip. "We haven't decided on the rooms yet. Just because you put up those ugly spotted curtains doesn't mean —"

"Yes, it does!"

"Does not!"

Daisy gave Katie a smile of sympathy as she was dragged upstairs by Rosehip *and* Bluebell.

As the three girls walked into the bedroom, Katie was amazed by what she saw. Bluebell had woven grass stems together to make a beautiful green patterned rug and painted bluebells on the wardrobe doors. She'd sewn two squares of material together and stuffed them with moss, to make a cozy comforter. There were a few

smaller rectangles of material laid carefully out on the bed, along with some dandelion petals, ready to be made into pillows. Flower stems were sticking out from under a chest of drawers, and when Katie tried to move it she discovered that it was very heavy — Bluebell had filled the drawers with stones! "I'm pressing some flowers to make pictures," Bluebell explained, "for *my* walls."

"How nice," said Katie, but Rosehip just stood with her hands on her hips and tossed her bright hair, eyes blazing. "They're not *your* walls! You know I want this room! I'm going to make a dandelion comforter and —"

"You can't!" shouted Bluebell. "I'm making pillowcases with polka dots on them, to match my curtains!"

"They're not *your* curtains!" Rosehip shouted back. Then suddenly

they lunged at each other and fell back onto the bed, in a furious flurry of wings and petals. Rosehip had grabbed Bluebell's leg, and Bluebell was pulling Rosehip's long flaming hair.

"Ow!"

"Youch!"

"Let go!"

"No, you first!"

"No, you!"

"Both of you stop that NOW!" Katie cried. The two fairies let go of each other and sat bolt upright, startled. Daisy and Snowdrop rushed into the room.

"Actually they're all *my* rooms," said Katie firmly. "And those curtains are made from *my* fabric! It's *my* dollhouse!"

All the fairies stared at her, shocked. "Sorry," muttered Bluebell. "We know it's your house really, because we saw you out here playing yesterday."

"That's why I felt like I was being watched!" said Katie. "It was you four!"

"Yes," said Daisy. "Then when you left the dollhouse outside, we just thought, well hoped really, that maybe, uh, that you'd forget all about it and we could stay here and —"

"We don't have anywhere else to go!" wailed Snowdrop.

"If you won't let us stay, we'll have to camp out under a big leaf!" said Rosehip, fuming, "and that is *no* fun in a thunderstorm, I can tell you!"

Katie smiled. "Calm down!" she said soothingly. "Of course you can stay here in the house, but no arguing, OK? You've got an important task to do!"

"OK," said Rosehip grudgingly. "I suppose Bluebell can have this room, seeing as she's already started decorating, but only if she helps me with the sewing on my dandelion bedspread."

"Deal," said Bluebell, and they shook hands, though Katie thought their grip was a bit harder than necessary!

Snowdrop and Daisy were easy to figure out. Being a summer fairy, Daisy wanted the other sunny room looking out on to the almost-meadow, while winter sprite Snowdrop wanted the darker, cooler room facing the oak tree.

When everything was sorted out, Snowdrop led Katie excitedly into her new room and climbed straight into the wardrobe, which she'd bewitched with fairy dust so that the doors really opened. "It's fantastic that you've gotten these big cupboards for playing hide-and-seek in," she said, smiling. "See!"

Katie couldn't help giggling. "They're for your clothes!" she cried.

"They're called wardrobes. Don't you have them in Fairyland?"

"But we're *wearing* our clothes," replied Snowdrop, looking confused.

The other fairies were all crowded in Snowdrop's doorway, listening.

"But when they get dirty you need to wash them, and then, when they're clean, you put them in the wardrobe," Katie explained.

"We only *have* these clothes," said Bluebell, twirling around to show off her blue petal skirt. "And anyway, fairies don't *get* dirty."

Katie grinned. "Lucky you! You won't be needing the bathtub either, then!"

"What's the bathtub?" asked Daisy.

"Do you mean that big potion-mixing pot in the little room?" asked Rosehip.

"Yes!" answered Katie, shaking with laughter. "It sounds like you've never been in a human house! You could come home with me if you want and see how wardrobes work, and bath-tubs, and I can show you *my* room —"

"Oh, no, we fairies never go inside

human houses," shrieked Snowdrop, with a shudder. "There's no fresh air, and we feel all cooped up, and we can't breathe, and it makes us go a bit . . . uh . . ."

"Crazy," finished Bluebell, boldly.

"Besides, we need to stay here and get to work making some fairy lights," said Daisy anxiously. "We hardly slept a wink last night. Fairies are scared of the dark, you see."

Katie nodded. Now *that* was something they had in common. She still needed the nightlight on in the hall, even though she was getting a little too old for nightlights.

"I know how we can make some lights," said Rosehip. "All we

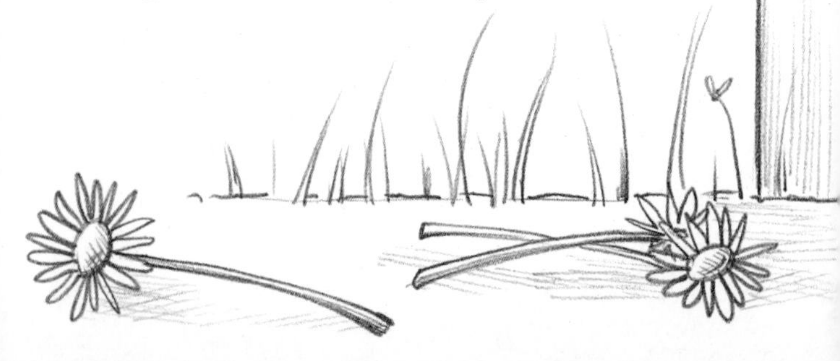

need are some flowers and a smidgeon of fairy dust!" She gave Daisy a wink and hurried down the stairs. Curious, they all followed her into the almost-meadow.

Once outside (and with Katie still on the lookout for buzzing bees!), they began picking daisies from the shorter grass by the wire fence. Katie could see her mom from there, sitting on the patio, engrossed in a book about Matisse, the painter.

Katie was glad she hadn't been missed. If she were suddenly called in, she'd have

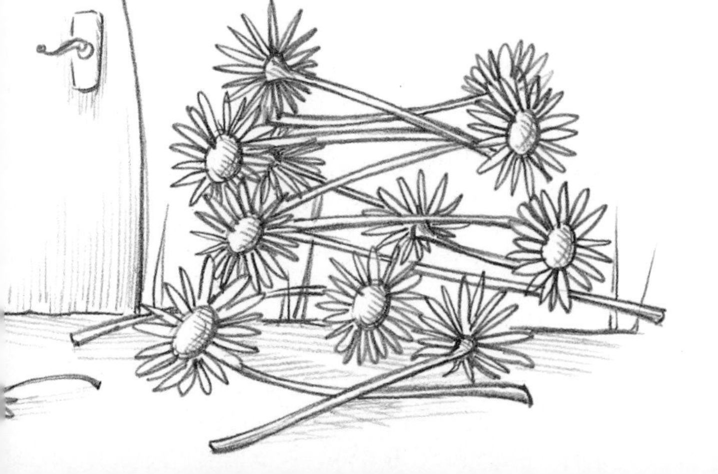

to hope that turning big again was just as quick as shrinking, so she could get back to the house before her mom came looking for her.

To the fairies, the daisies were the size of brooms, and they could only hold a couple at a time. It was hard work, but soon they'd collected a big pile by the front door.

"Now we just need to take them inside the house and light them," said Rosehip. "But, oh, how will we hang them up?"

Katie smiled. "We could make them into a long daisy chain!" she suggested. "It's so much fun, and then they'll be easy to put up!"

"Great idea!" said Bluebell enthusiastically. "Uh, what's a daisy chain?"

So Katie showed the fairies how to thread the daisy stems together.

"You're right, this *is* fun!" cried Rosehip, as the chain grew and grew. But after a while they got very uncomfortable and fidgety sitting on the bumpy tree roots, so Bluebell gathered up some twigs and made a bench long enough for five. Katie held her breath as they all sat down, but the long strands of grass woven around the twigs held the bench firmly together. While they added more and more daisies to the chain, Rosehip taught Katie a fairy song, then Katie taught them the one about the kookaburra.

As they sang, Katie thought about how lonely she'd felt the day before, singing all by herself, and when they finished, she couldn't help saying, "I really hope you'll be my friends."

Daisy grinned, dropped her part of

the chain into her lap, and gave Katie a big hug. "We hope you'll be ours, too!" she said happily. Then all the fairies joined in the hug and some of the daisies got a bit squashed, but no one minded.

When the daisy chain was ready, Snowdrop went to get the bottle of fairy dust from the kitchen table. She

shook some of the glittering powder into her hand and sprinkled it onto the daisy at the very end of the chain. It shrunk down to exactly the perfect size, and then the middle of each daisy began to glow softly, warm and welcoming and bright enough to chase away any shadows in the night. Katie squealed, amazed.

"It works!" cried Bluebell, and they all clapped and cheered and danced around in a big circle to celebrate.

Then they took the daisy chain inside and strung it all over the house, from room to room and in and out of the windows. "Just the kitchen to go now," said Katie.

"What's a kitchen?" asked Snowdrop.

Bluebell jumped up and down with her hand in the air, crying, "I know! I know! Is it that strange room with the

big table and all the empty drawers and cupboards? We've been trying to figure out what it's for!"

"It's for making your food and eating it!" Katie laughed. "How can you not know that? Surely you must *eat*! Food keeps you alive . . . and it's delicious!"

"We fairies live on love and laughter," said Snowdrop. "We don't have food in Fairyland."

"Oh!" said Katie, smiling. "So your mouth must only be for talking! No wonder you have so many arguments!"

"Aren't you fresh!" cried Rosehip — with a grin.

Katie beamed — this was just like having real friends, friends that you could tease and be silly with and help when they had a problem.

Suddenly, Katie caught a glimpse

of her watch. "Oh, no, I've to go! If I'm late for lunch my mom will come looking for me, and if she can't see me she'll worry and —"

"But what about the fairy task?" cried Bluebell. "We haven't even started to figure it out —"

"I have to go now," Katie interrupted. "But I'll find out what these birthstone things are — promise." She looked at Daisy in panic. "But how do I . . ." she began.

"Don't worry," said Daisy gently, "just touch the door handle and say the spell again, then you'll turn big."

So Katie gave all the fairies a quick hug and hurried

out of the door. Then she put her little finger on the door handle and whispered, "I believe in fairies. I believe in fairies. I believe in fairies."

This time it was her toes that fizzed and crackled, and then suddenly everything seemed to be getting smaller as she grew to her normal size. When she glanced down, the wooden bench Bluebell had made looked tiny. She could hardly believe that she'd actually been *sitting* on it!

"Bye!" she called, and four little fairy heads popped out of Bluebell's bedroom window to wave at her. Katie couldn't help smiling as she picked her way through the grass and wild flowers to the wire fence. "I made some new friends," she whispered to herself. "And they're fairies! Who would ever believe it?!" For the

first time since the move, she felt truly happy.

But as she dashed across the yard and hurried in for lunch, she had no idea that disaster was about to strike.

Of course, her mom didn't mean to spoil everything. As she served the macaroni and cheese and tried to pile salad onto Katie's plate, she simply said, "Oh, darling, we both forgot about bringing your dollhouse inside last night. Could you be sure to remember it today? It would be such a shame if it got ruined."

Katie froze, her forkful of pasta hovering halfway to her mouth. She hadn't even *thought* of that — that her mom might want her to bring the dollhouse inside. But how could she? Not now that she'd given each of the fairies a room and said they could

stay, and after they'd become her new friends and everything. "But I can't," she blurted out.

Katie's mom raised her eyebrows. "Why not?" she asked, a little snappily. "I know that dollhouse wasn't the exact one you wanted, but I thought you'd take better care of it than this! I'm not made of money, Katie."

Katie's stomach lurched and she pushed her salad around on her plate. She suddenly didn't feel hungry anymore. She hated that her mom was upset about her leaving the dollhouse outside. Maybe if she explained, told the truth — well, there was a tiny chance her mom might believe her. She took a deep breath. "I can't bring the dollhouse in because there are fairies living in it . . ." she began.

But her mom just frowned. "Oh Katie, don't be silly. I'm being serious now," she said, crossly. "I want that dollhouse brought in."

Katie bowed her head, blinking back tears. They ate the rest of their lunch in silence.

Afterward Katie went right upstairs and read on her own until dinner time.

She was so upset she hardly even bothered looking at the pictures, and she turned the pages so hard that one ripped. Her mind whirled with questions — Where would the poor fairies go? How would she tell them? Would they be angry, or even stop being friends with her? Katie wondered whether they'd still let her do the task with them. Even if she did find out what birthstones were, would they still *want* her help? They might not, not after she let them down so terribly. Oh, it was all such a mess!

At dinner time, she sat with her food on her lap, watching TV, trying not to think about the dollhouse. It was all her mom's fault! Oh, why wouldn't she just believe her?

But Katie couldn't be angry with her mom. After all, she didn't know

the truth about the dollhouse, so she didn't know what she was asking. And besides, Katie hated it when they argued. So, when her mom came up to kiss her good night, Katie gave her a big hug and tried to look happy.

"Have you brought it in yet?" her mom asked.

"Oh, I'm sorry, I forgot again," said Katie, though it wasn't quite true. "And now I'm ready for bed."

Her mom sighed. "I'll have to go and get it then," she muttered.

Katie grabbed her arm, panic in her eyes. "Oh, no, please don't," she begged. "I'll bring it in tomorrow morning, first thing, before school — I promise."

"OK, then," said her mom, giving her a puzzled look. "But make sure you do, or you'll be in trouble!"

Once her mom had gone downstairs, Katie got up again and looked out of the window. She could just about see over to the oak tree. The daisy lights glowed dimly in the dollhouse beneath it. The fairies must be wondering why she hadn't come back out. She'd put off the awful moment for as long as possible, but

deep down she knew that she had no choice — if *she* didn't bring the doll-house in, her *mom* would.

Either way, she was about to lose her new friends forever.

Chapter 4

Katie lingered over her cornflakes the next day, as her mom did some dishes at the sink.

"I'm sorry you're still upset, darling," said Katie's mom wearily. "But I meant what I said. If you don't go and get that dollhouse and bring it in before school, I'll do it myself."

"I'll go right now," said Katie, leaving her cereal bowl half-full. She pulled on her shoes and crossed the dewy lawn. Her legs felt weighed

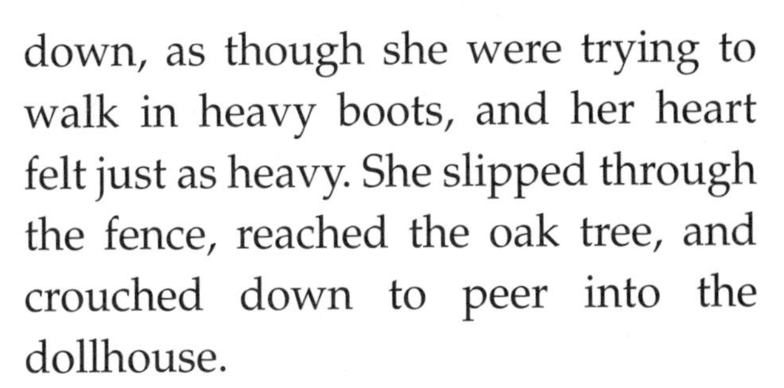

down, as though she were trying to walk in heavy boots, and her heart felt just as heavy. She slipped through the fence, reached the oak tree, and crouched down to peer into the dollhouse.

Bluebell and Rosehip were having a polka-dot pillow fight on Bluebell's bed, giggling and squealing. Daisy was flying around adjusting the fairy lights they'd made together. Pink

and purple flowers now grew from window boxes made of woven grass. Just then, Snowdrop leaned out of the living room window, holding a tiny watering can made from an acorn cup, and began watering one of them.

"Hi, Katie," she called, breathless with excitement. "Do you like my flowers?" Katie nodded miserably, but Snowdrop didn't realize that anything was wrong and kept chatting away. "You should have come back yesterday — we missed you so much! Daisy's going to paint her room today so she wants to know which shade of yellow you like best, and Rosehip's got another fairy song to teach you, and Bluebell made up this great game but we need five to play it and —"

Katie sighed heavily. "I can't," she mumbled. "I've got school, and I've also got some very bad news."

Soon, a shrunk-down Katie was standing in the kitchen of the dollhouse, with the four fairies gathered around her, all looking as completely miserable as she did.

"I'm so sorry," she said again, "but I've got no choice. My mom insisted that I bring the dollhouse in. I tried to explain about you, but she just wouldn't believe me. I'm so, so sorry."

"It's OK," mumbled Daisy, trying to smile. "It's not your fault."

"Yes it is!" cried Bluebell suddenly, making Snowdrop jump.

"That's right!" added Rosehip, making her tiny hands into fists in anger. "*You* promised we could stay

here! A promise is a promise and I'm not leaving, so there!"

"But . . ." began Katie.

"Me, neither!" cried Bluebell. "You can't make us!"

"No, you can't make us!" echoed Snowdrop, startling everyone. Looking determined, she grabbed hold of the kitchen table and held on. Bluebell and Rosehip liked this idea and leaped across the room to attach themselves to the kitchen cupboards with the tiebacks Bluebell had made for her polka-dot curtains.

"Look, I'm as upset as you are," said Katie, indignantly. "But it's *my* dollhouse and if I ask you to go you should go!" She glanced at Daisy for help but she just mumbled, "I'm not leaving all by myself," and clutched a chair, avoiding Katie's glare.

"This is ridiculous!" Katie cried. "I

have to go to school in half an hour and I need to bring the dollhouse inside, so please get out now!"

But the fairies just held on tighter. Rosehip started a chant of *No, no, we will not go!* and the others soon joined in. Then Bluebell stuck her tongue out at Katie, which was the final straw.

Katie lunged at Bluebell and pulled at her wrist. But Bluebell just held on tight, kicking and squealing. Katie managed to pull Snowdrop off the table, but when she loosened her grip to make a grab for Daisy, Snowdrop wriggled away and wrapped herself tightly around a table leg like a koala. Katie started pulling at Rosehip then, but Bluebell leaned across and pinched her ribs until she had to let go. The four little fairies were a lot stronger than they looked! Katie realized that there was only one way to deal

with them. She got up from the floor and dusted herself off. "Fine!" she shouted. "You can stay where you are, then! But the dollhouse is coming inside!"

And with that she marched out of the door, grabbed the door handle, and said the magic words. Soon she was her normal size and easily able to pick up the whole dollhouse — fairies or no fairies. With her other hand she picked up her pencil case and bag of fabric scraps, then marched back toward the house.

"No, Katie, please!" Daisy called through the kitchen window. "You know fairies don't like going inside human houses."

"Tough luck," said Katie, fuming. "You wouldn't get out, so now you're going in!"

"But being in your house will make us get very, very —" began Rosehip, but Katie wasn't listening.

Once inside, she set the dollhouse down on the table.

"Are you coming?" she called up to her mom.

"OK, just putting on some makeup," came the reply from the bathroom. Katie suddenly remembered her mom's interview in town about showing some of her paintings in the local gallery. She didn't usually bother with makeup so Katie knew it must be important.

She peered into the dollhouse. Snowdrop was still clinging angrily to the table leg, but Rosehip and Bluebell had run upstairs and hidden under Bluebell's comforter. Daisy was leaning out of the living room window, setting a crooked flower box

straight. "Please, Daisy, just come out," Katie begged, one last time.

But it wasn't Daisy who answered. It was Bluebell. She threw off the comforter and stood up on the bed, hands on hips. "Fine, we will," she called, pouting.

But if Katie had known what was about to happen, she'd have begged them to stay inside the dollhouse after all!

Bluebell stepped out of the front door onto a pile of magazines, then she screeched and shot into the air as they slid onto the floor with a great *whumph*!

Rosehip tiptoed out and looked around. "So this is what it's like to be indoors," she said with a gasp.

Daisy and Snowdrop came out behind her, staring in amazement.

"See, it's not so bad," said Katie,

crouching down to gather up the magazines. "Maybe you could live in the dollhouse inside my house and . . ."

But suddenly all the fairies started panting and fidgeting and scratching themselves.

"It's too stuffy in here," said Daisy, wheezing. "I can't breathe. Must have air . . ." And with that, she flew across the room and jumped both feet down on the switch of the electric fan, which was sitting in a corner.

The fan started up, its head whizzing one way and then the other. Katie gasped as it blew a pile of papers on the windowsill, sent them flying into the air, and then blew them all around the room. She dropped the magazines and ran around, trying to grab the papers. She glanced nervously at the stairs, but her mom had the hairdryer going, so at least she couldn't hear all the noise. Katie hoped that there was time to straighten everything up before she came down.

"Help me clean up this mess!" she ordered the fairies, but they ignored her.

"You made us come inside," said Rosehip, "so it serves you right!" She flew down to the floor, where Katie's toy ponies were lying in front of the television, and mounted an orange one.

"Catch," called Snowdrop, pulling the bottle of fairy dust from her pocket and throwing it to Rosehip. In one move Rosehip plucked the bottle out of the air, pulled out the cork, and sprinkled fairy dust on the plastic pony. It suddenly came to life and galloped over an armchair and onto the table, through Katie's mom's paints and across her latest picture, leaving little colored hoof prints all over it. "Stop!" cried Katie, but Rosehip just urged the pony on, around and around the canvas, ruining the painting.

"That looks like fun!" cried Snowdrop, diving down to the abandoned fairy-dust bottle and bringing

a white unicorn to life for herself. "Yee-hah!" she shouted, jumping aboard and galloping along the arm of the sofa. The unicorn's horn knocked over a mug that was balanced there. As it smashed on the wooden floor, cold coffee spilled over a pile of magazines and papers.

"Stop it!" Katie cried, but no one even heard her. That was because Bluebell was jumping on the volume button of the TV remote control so that the voices and music got louder and louder and louder.

Katie stared in horror at the chaos around her. How could they do this to her? They were supposed to be her friends! She just couldn't

stand it! She clamped her hands over her ears and screamed her loudest, most shriekingly ear-splitting scream.

That's when Katie's mom dashed in. She grabbed the remote control and turned off the TV, but she didn't seem to see Bluebell tumbling through the air. The ponies, just toys again, thudded to the floor.

Katie took her hands away from her

ears and gaped at her mother. The room was a disaster area. How could she even *begin* to explain? The only thing she could try was telling the truth. "It was the fairies, Mom," she blurted out. "Please, you've got to believe me. It really was! I tried to get them out of the dollhouse, so I could bring it in like you said, but —"

"How could you do this?" shouted Katie's mom, stopping Katie dead. "My painting's ruined! I was taking it with me to the gallery. It's my best work! How could you do all this, just because I asked you to bring that dollhouse in?"

Katie's mom stared at Katie, waiting for an answer, but she felt so awful she couldn't say anything at all.

"I'm very disappointed in you, Katie," her mom continued. "Now clean this all up, this instant!" And

with that she stormed back upstairs, slamming the living room door behind her.

Katie stood stunned, her knees trembling and her stomach flipping over and over. She'd hardly ever seen her mom so angry. She collapsed onto the sofa and started to cry.

Chapter 5

All of a sudden, Katie felt four little fairies land in her lap. She blinked at them through her tears, but they wouldn't meet her eye; they were all hanging their heads in shame.

"Katie, we're so sorry," said Daisy, eventually. "I don't know what got into us. We didn't mean to make so much trouble — we were just so angry and upset about losing our new home and friend, and we hate being in human houses!"

"I noticed!" Katie sniffled.

"We'll go now," said Bluebell sadly. "We've caused enough trouble."

"We really are sorry," said Rosehip.

"Yes, we really are," echoed Snowdrop.

And with that all the fairies flew into the air, toward the open back door.

Katie suddenly sat upright. "Wait," she called, "I think I have an idea. If we can make the house even cleaner than it was before, it would show my mom how sorry I am. And if I can make her understand how much I want to keep the dollhouse outside, there's a tiny chance she'll let me. But we have to be quick — I leave for school soon. And it means being inside for a little bit longer."

"We can handle another few minutes," said Bluebell, taking some deep breaths.

"We should be able to do it before your mom comes back down — with a little sprinkle of fairy dust to help us," added Snowdrop.

"Then let's go!" cried Katie, leaping to her feet. And with that they all started whirling around the room, cleaning and tidying. Daisy turned off the fan, Rosehip and Bluebell got a sponge from the kitchen sink and flew back and forth over the coffee spill, soaking it up. Katie collected the papers and placed them firmly under a paperweight,

then scooped the magazines back onto the table, while Snowdrop fixed the painting, dabbing fairy dust on each tiny painted hoof print so that it vanished.

Then, in the kitchen, Daisy and Snowdrop helped Katie make her lunch, while Rosehip and Bluebell painted a "Sorry" card with Katie's mom's paints.

Katie's mom opened the door just as Bluebell was finishing the Y on *Sorry*. Bluebell squeaked and quickly dropped the paintbrush back into its pot so that Katie's mom wouldn't see it hovering in midair!

When Katie came through from the kitchen, lunch box in hand, Rosehip tugged at her arm and pointed to the card. Katie smiled, picked it up and held it out to her mom. "I'm so sorry I made such a mess," she said.

Her mom sighed deeply and took the card. "What am I going to do with you?" she muttered. Then she pulled Katie into a big hug and added, "I shouldn't have been so hard on you. I'm just a bit stressed out this morning — this gallery meeting is so important."

"I know — I'm so sorry. But I fixed your painting."

"Wow!" cried her mom. "How did you do that?"

But Katie decided it was best not to answer. Instead she took a deep breath and twisted her ring nervously around her finger. "Mom," she said carefully, "well, you know how important the gallery meeting is to you? It's just . . . if something was that important to *me*, would you think about allowing it?"

Her mom smiled. "Well, I'd have to know what the thing was first," she said gently.

"I'd like to keep the dollhouse under the oak tree," Katie barely whispered, hardly daring to hope. "You see, I'm making it into a home for the fairies, and fairies can't live indoors."

Before her mom could say no, Katie led her over to the dollhouse and clicked the latch open so that it folded out like a book. Then she showed her everything they'd done inside — pretending it was all her own work, of course! "Look, I've already made little bedspreads and curtains and rugs for them," she explained, "and window boxes with flowers and . . ."

"Wow, they're beautiful!" Katie's mom gasped. "What a gorgeous shade of purple."

"I'm even painting this room yellow," Katie continued, pointing into Daisy's bedroom. "I've mixed a few different shades, and I'm going to decide which is the nicest." Daisy was hovering by the back door and Katie caught her eye. The little fairy waved her crossed fingers in the air hopefully.

Katie's mom looked at everything very carefully, even though Katie was almost late for school. "Wow, Katie, you really have done a wonderful job of making this your very own," she said. "I'm so sorry, darling. I didn't understand. I thought you'd left the dollhouse outside because you didn't care about it, but I can see now that you really do."

"So can I put it back under the oak tree?" asked Katie. She held her breath and watched the fairies hovering, fingers crossed, eyes squeezed shut.

"Yes," said her mom. "In fact, let's go and put it there right now."

Katie grinned and gave her mom a big hug, saying "Thank you, thank you, thank you," into her ear. Then she clicked the dollhouse shut and together they took it back out to the

tree, the fairies following along at Katie's shoulder, twirling and dancing in the air.

Katie placed the dollhouse carefully on the ground and the gleeful fairies landed on the roof. "See you after school," she whispered to them.

"Who are you talking to?" asked her mom.

Katie started. "Oh, uh, just the fairies," she said.

"That's such a nice game, darling," said her mom, taking Katie's hand. "What a wonderful imagination you have. And what are the names of these fairies?"

And so, as they headed back to the house, Katie told her mom all about Bluebell, Rosehip, Snowdrop, and Daisy, knowing that she wouldn't believe a single word!

Chapter 6

Katie tugged at her mom's hand all the way back from school, almost making her run down the street! She'd looked up birthstones in the library during their quiet reading time and made a list of them — and she'd found, to her amazement, that she already had one! As soon as they got home she threw down her book bag and ran out to the dollhouse. Once there, she checked that her mom wasn't looking, but she didn't need to

worry — the gallery meeting had been a great success and her mom was busy inside doing some rough sketches for new paintings.

Katie put her little finger on the tiny blue door handle and closed her eyes. "I believe in fairies. I believe in fairies. I believe in fairies," she whispered. With a tingling at the top of her head and the strange feeling that everything around her was getting bigger, she shrank down to fairy size.

The fairies came dashing out of the dollhouse to meet her and they all hugged. Katie felt happiness welling up inside her — it was just so wonderful that everything was back to normal and they were all friends again!

"I've got a —" she began, but Daisy was tugging at her hand and jumping around with excitement. "Come and

pick a yellow for my room!" she said. "I've been waiting for you all day! These girls are hopeless — we can't agree on which shade — and anyway, Bluebell keeps saying it should be blue!"

"Bluebell thinks *everything* should be blue!" Rosehip laughed.

So they all ran inside and together Katie and Daisy picked out the most

cheerful, sunshiny yellow of all. They got to work with her paints and brushes, which were as big as brooms in their tiny hands, and soon every wall was yellow! Then Katie went to help Bluebell put the finishing touches on her new room (which was all blue, of course!).

"Oh, we just need the curtain tie-backs," said Bluebell. She blushed a

deep pink and said, "They're still in the kitchen from when we, uh, well, when we tied ourselves to the cupboards."

Katie smiled. "I'll get them," she said, to show that there were no bad feelings. She went running down the stairs just like she did in her own house. As she picked up the tiebacks from the kitchen table, the sunlight coming in through the window caught her ring, lighting it up with a red flash. She suddenly remembered the exciting news she had to tell her friends.

She raced back upstairs and went crashing into Daisy's room. "I found out what birthstones are!" she cried breathlessly, as all the fairies gathered around in excitement. "They're different gems, and each one is linked to a month of the year. I made a list of them." She rummaged in her pocket

and pulled out the piece of paper she'd written them down on, and they all read it. "There's diamond and pearl and opal and topaz and so many more!" squealed Snowdrop.

"Now that we know what to look for we can get started on the fairy task!" cried Daisy.

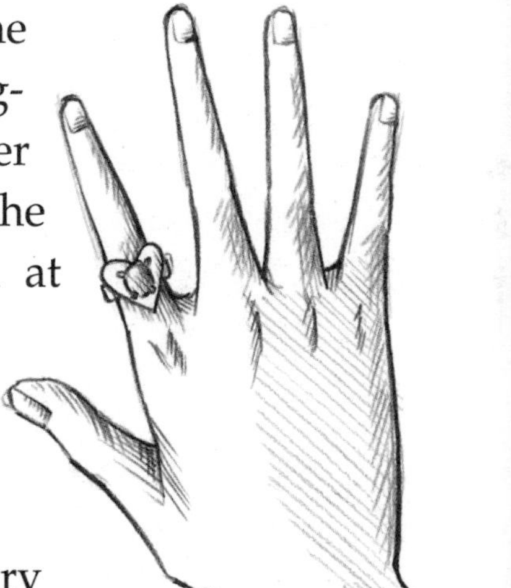

Katie beamed. "Even better, I've got one already!" She giggled, waving her hand in the air. The fairies all peered at the ring that Aunt Jane had given her. "It's a garnet," she told them, "the January birthstone. My birthday's not in January, but Aunt Jane's is. She gave this to me because it got too small for her when she grew up!"

The fairies all jumped up and down, squealing with excitement.

"See, the Fairy Queen wants you to succeed, just like Daisy said," reasoned Katie. "She must have known I had the right gemstone! Maybe she sort of made me forget the dollhouse that first night, so that we'd meet and I'd give you the first birthstone!"

"So she does care after all!" cried Snowdrop.

"Maybe we really *can* do this task," said Rosehip.

"But, Katie, will you help us?" asked Daisy.

"Of course — you're my friends," said Katie. "We have to save the tree together. The person planning to knock it down must be a builder of

some kind — I'm sure I can find out who it is and what he's up to. Then we'll know how long we've got to make the magic work." Katie twisted the garnet ring around her finger. "And I'll take extra good care of this from now on."

"Now we just have to find all the other birthstones," said Snowdrop, frowning.

"Let's wait until tomorrow," said Katie. "We made a good start, and besides, it's almost time for me to go, and I still haven't seen what you did with the rest of the house!"

So the fairies gave Katie the grand tour and showed her all their work. Bluebell's beautiful pressed-flower pictures hung on the walls, and Snowdrop's window boxes had sprouted twice as many blooms

under her loving care. The living room had been transformed with rose-petal covers on the sofas, and Rosehip had shaken a dash of fairy dust onto the plastic piano so that it really worked.

"You've made the dollhouse really perfect," Katie exclaimed. "But it just needs one more thing."

She headed upstairs, smiling a mysterious smile, and returned with one of the paintbrushes from Daisy's room. They all followed her outside, curious, and watched as she painted

The Fairy House

on the front door in beautiful curly lettering. Then she turned to the fairies and smiled. "It's not a dollhouse anymore — it's the Fairy House now,"

she declared. "I'm giving it to you. Welcome to your new home!"

"Oh, wow!" they all cried, grabbing her in hugs. "Thank you, thank you, thank you!"

Beaming, Katie hugged her new friends back, as hard as she could. "Will you play the piano for us, Rosehip?" she asked, when they finally broke apart.

"I'd love to!" cried Rosehip.

Soon, beautiful tinkling music filled the Fairy House, and they all joined in the fairy song, dancing and singing and whirling and spinning and laughing, just like real friends do.

The End

Bluebell
Spring fairy

Likes:

blue, blue, blue, and more blue,
doing somersaults in the air, dancing

Dislikes:

finishing second, being told what to do

Daisy
Summer fairy

Likes:

everyone to be friends, bright sunshine,
cheery yellow colors, smiling

Dislikes:

arguments, cold dark places,
ugly orange dresses

Rosehip

Autumn fairy

Likes:

riding magic ponies, telling Bluebell what to do, playing the piano, singing

Dislikes:

keeping quiet, boring colors, not being the center of attention!

Snowdrop

Winter fairy

Likes:

singing fairy songs, cool quiet places, riding her favorite magical unicorn, making snowfairies

Dislikes:

being too hot, keeping secrets

Don't miss the rest of the series!

The Fairy House
Fairy for a Day
Bluebell
x
Kelly McKain

The Fairy House
Fairy Riding School
Rosehip x
Kelly McKain

The Fairy House
Fairies to the Rescue
Daisy
Kelly McKain